FIRST SPRING

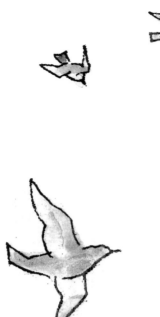

To my parents
– G. C.

To all storytellers
who keep alive the
legends and tales that
make us human.
– R. S. and C. G.

Published in 2006 by Simply Read Books
www.simplyreadbooks.com

First published in French by Les 400 Coups

Text © 2006 Rémi Savard, Catherine Germain
Illustrations © 2006 Geneviève Côté
Translation © 2006 Donald Kellough

Library and Archives Canada Cataloguing in Publication
Savard, Rémi, 1934-
[Premier printemps du monde. English]
First spring: an Innu tale of North America / Rémi Savard, Catherine
Germain ; illustrations by Geneviève Côté ; translated by Donald Kellough.
Translation of: Le premier printemps du monde.
For children.
ISBN 1-894965-34-5
ISBN-13 978-1-894965-34-7
1. Seasons – Juvenile fiction. I. Germain, Catherine, 1944-
II. Côté, Geneviève, 1964- III. Kellough, Donald IV. Title.
PS8587.A38772P7313 2006   jC843'.54   C2005-906985-6

Design: Mathilde Herbert and Jody de Haas
Editors: Louise Chabalier and James Hunt

Printed in China

10 9 8 7 6 5 4 3 2 1

We acknowledge the support of the Canada Council for the Arts for our publishing program.

FIRST SPRING

AN INNU TALE OF NORTH AMERICA

RÉMI SAVARD & CATHERINE GERMAIN
***with* ILLUSTRATIONS *by:* GENEVIÈVE CÔTÉ**

Simply Read Books

Back in the days when this story took place,
a long, long time ago, the seasons did not yet exist.
The ancestors of today's human beings
knew only winter, snow, cold and night.

In those days, the different forms of life
were more alike than unlike.
Human beings and animals had not yet grown apart
and indeed could speak each other's language.

One day, a pair of these somewhat human, somewhat animal
beings set out to join a caribou hunting party.
They were travelling with their only little one in tow, but along
the way, they decided to abandon him.
He was covered with lice, or so they claimed, and
he kept them from sleeping as he tossed and turned and
scratched himself the whole night through!
So, one morning, they ran off without him.

The little one saw them leave. He ran after them
in the snow but could not catch up with them.
He then turned around and walked until he reached the bed of
spruce branches on which he had slept the night before.
There he sat down all alone, and cried.

A while later, someone heard him crying all alone
and came to his rescue. The sight of the enormous,
hairy creature made the little one scream out in terror:

"Mama, mama! I'm scared!
Atshen the ogre is going to eat me!"

"I am not Atshen. But now tell me something, why did your
parents go off and abandon you?" the giant asked him.

"Because I had lice!" the little one replied.

"Come now, loving parents do not abandon their little
one because he has lice!" chided the giant who was, in fact,
Mistapeo, the Great Spirit, the one who brings food
to all living things creatures.

Mistapeo took the little one into his arms and gently,
oh so gently, removed the lice.
He made sure, however, to leave one family of lice behind.

"One day," he said, "When the weather is finer and
human beings inhabit the earth, this will help to keep them busy."

Then, Mistapeo dropped the little one into one of his mittens and
set out to bring him to his parents. Some say that the little one put
on an entire caribou hide that his mother had left behind.
It made a splendid little suit for him, with the caribou head even
providing him with a hood. Indeed, when he had his suit on,
the little one looked very much like a small caribou.

Along the way, they spotted a young porcupine.

"Kill him, Grandfather, and I'll roast him."

"No, no, my little one. He is still a little too little.
There will be other ones. One must always treat the
young with care so that life may continue.

Later, they came upon a bigger porcupine, which Mistapeo
agreed to kill. The little one then roasted it just as he had promised.
When the meat was done just right, he asked Mistapeo which
special piece he wanted to eat.

"No, I won't be having any roasted porcupine," said the
Great Spirit, "Since any piece I eat would leave that
much less for living things to enjoy. No one likes the lungs,
so they will be just fine for me." Indeed, if it weren't for
Mistapeo's generosity, no one today would have any game to eat.

As soon as they arrived at the parents' camp site, Mistapeo set down the little one, who ran ahead to their tent and stepped inside.

"Who brought you here?" his parents gasped.

"Grandfather did. Take a look outside."

The father opened the door a crack, then shouted out in fear: "It's Atshen who has brought him here. Atshen is going to eat us alive!"

"If anyone here resembles Atshen, it is more likely to be you," exclaimed Mistapeo. "You abandoned your little one to the hungry lice!" Then, shrinking to a size allowing him to enter the tent, he protested: "How can you mistake **me**, who provides food to living creatures, with the ogre who eats them?"

Mistapeo stayed inside the tent a while,
since he did not wish to accompany the hunters.
Most especially, he did not want to eat any of the game
that they were sure to bring back with them – only
those few pieces of lung that no one else wanted.

During this time, the woman stayed behind
at the camp alone. She wondered why Mistapeo
had not gone hunting with the others.
She also wondered why he remained without stirring:
"He doesn't even step outside to answer the call of nature!"

Mistapeo knew what she was thinking and so he decided that the
time had come for him to leave.

"I'll be moving along, then," he said. "This time, take
good care of the little one. He'll be very sad to find out that
I've gone. Do everything you can to comfort him.
Children are the future of living creatures!"

But how could they have understood what he meant,
since they had no experience of death?

When he got back from the hunt, the little one asked:
"Where's grandfather?"

"He has gone," they replied.

"I'll go and catch up with him," he declared.

His parents tried to hold him back, but he was able to escape.

The great Mistapeo saw the child running up to him from behind.

He scooped him up, sat him upright in the palm of his hand, and then, with a mighty puff, blew him back to his parents. The child plopped down to earth right in front of the family tent and burst into tears at once. He cried and cried until he was nearly out of breath.

His parents wondered: "What could we possibly give the little one to comfort him?"
They didn't know very much about anything, aside from winter, cold and night. Though it was true that they had already heard tell of another land where there was always light and warmth – a place where summer was never ending.

"I would stop crying," said the little one, "If I could catch some small birds of summer with an arrow."

"What makes you think you could do something that so many others have failed to do before you! Light and warmth are elsewhere, far, far away in the lands to the south. That is where the birds of summer are found."

But though the way south was quite uncertain, early one morning
they decided to head out all the same.
Many creatures came along with them, including several who would
one day become men and women, and others,
like Caribou, Beaver, Fox or Otter, who would one day
become animals.

All these creatures of the night and the cold then struck out for
the south – for the lands of light and warmth. There they planned to steal
away the birds of summer from another group of creatures that had, from
the earliest times, enjoyed the birds all to themselves.

And so they walked,
and walked,
and walked.

Along their way, they stopped at the home of two old women.

"Where are you going?" the two old women asked.

"We are heading toward summer, for the little one
has been crying and crying and is nearly out of breath."

"Oh, what an adventure! Others before you have tried
and failed, but you are welcome to try again. Along your way,
you will meet Giant Beaver. He is very hospitable
and will offer to share some of his fat for you to eat. But there is
one thing you must remember. You must not laugh when
he begins to fart, for he is a very sensitive fellow.
If you laugh, he will take back his fat and store it away
in his knapsack. If that should happen, then stand to
each side of the doorway and have your knives ready.
When Giant Beaver steps out of his house,
you'll only need to cut the straps of the knapsack."

The old women also gave them advice about a giant whom
they would find lying across their path.
The road to summer was truly full of obstacles!

They were greeted by Giant Beaver
in front of his lodge. He asked them where they were going.

"We are trying to reach summer," declared
all the creatures of winter,"For a little one has been
crying and crying and is nearly out of breath."

"What an adventure!" exclaimed Giant Beaver.

He then took the fat out of his knapsack, cut it into pieces and handed
them around to his guests. But with each movement he made, he farted
aloud. Otter was unable to keep himself from laughing, which annoyed
Giant Beaver terribly. He immediately put the fat back into his knapsack
and headed out the door. At that point, Caribou and Fisher, who had
been waiting outside with sharpened knives, cut the straps of the
knapsack and made off with the fat without Giant Beaver ever noticing.

"Giant Beaver," the winter creatures shouted to him as they started on
their way again, "If ever the ice in your river starts to turn yellow and go
soft, this will be your proof that we succeeded."

Then they walked for a long long time until
they reached a huge cliff
blocking the way ahead of them.

They had run up against the leg of the giant, who was stretched
out over the ground and who was so big they could not
even see his head. So they sat down and
ate some of Giant Beaver's fat, all the while wondering
aloud how they were going to get around this obstacle.

They then began to jab at his leg with their spears,
just as the two old women had told them to.
"Until now no one has tried that," the women had told them.
All of a sudden, the huge leg budged, and a deep voice groaned:

"Ouch! Ouch! Stop and I'll open a passage,
so the little one won't cry anymore!"

They decided to pass under the giant's leg.
First, they greased up White Fox,
who dug a tunnel beneath.
Then, all the others followed him, each one
widening the tunnel on his way through.

After emerging on the other side, they continued on their way.
They followed a flowing river, certain that it would lead
them onward to where the birds and creatures of summer dwelled.
And sure enough, just before nightfall, whom did they see
floating along with the ice-free current but Muskrat!

The creatures of winter threw bits of fat to him
in hopes of making him a helpful friend of theirs. Muskrat dove
down into the water. He nibbled at the bits of fat,
occasionally licking his paws.

"Muskrat, tell us about the creatures of summer.
What do they do in the evening?"

"They have themselves a party," said Muskrat, "And they
dance. Life for the summer creatures is a never ending
feast. They sleep away the morning, but they have
two old women posted as lookouts."

"And where are the birds of summer?" they asked.

"At the bottom of a bag, at the back of the tent."

They then decided upon a strategy. At dawn, after they had made
holes in the canoes of the summer creatures
and had gnawed down their paddles, Muskrat would swim along
with the river, pushing a tree trunk ahead of him.
The two old women would be tricked into thinking that
the tree roots were the antlers of a moose,
and would raise a cry to begin the hunt.

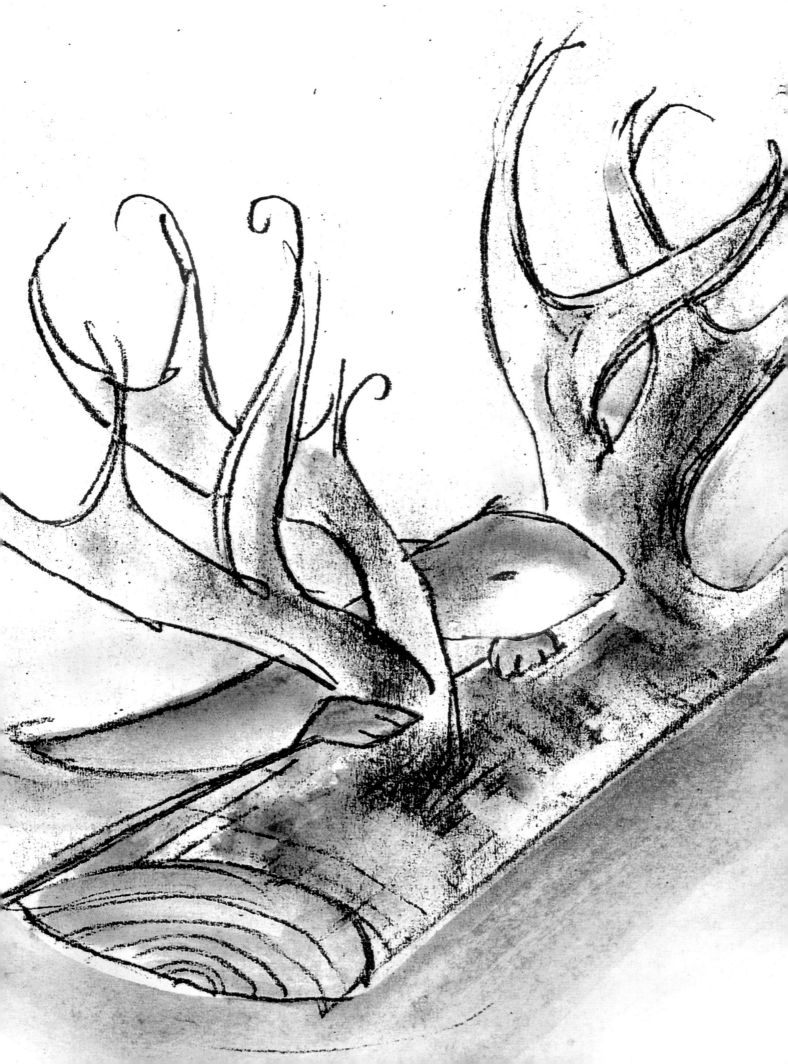

Everything happened just as they had planned.

Startled awake by the cries of the two old women,
the creatures of summer ran to their canoes
in hopes of catching the moose.
Some of them sank in the river while others
were set adrift, floating without a paddle.

Taking advantage of this chaos, the creatures of winter
rushed into the tent, grabbed the bag at the back,
and ran off. The bag holding all the birds of summer
was passed to the two fastest members of the group –
Fisher and Caribou.

Meanwhile, the two old women
could be heard shrieking over
and over again
to those in the river who
were struggling to avoid
disaster:

"They have snatched
summer away from us!

They have snatched summer
away from us!"

While still dripping wet, the creatures of summer took
off in hot pursuit of the thieves. They were so quick,
those creatures of summer, that they soon managed to run over
Otter and then Loon. That is why, even to this day, the flanks of
both these creatures are flat.

Seeing that the summer creatures were catching up,
Fisher volunteered to slow them down, so he climbed
to the top of a white spruce.

"We've caught another one," shouted the creatures of
summer. "And, what's more, he's supposed to be the fastest
one in their group! But there he is, up high in that tree.
So now, where is our champion archer?"

As the archer was slow in coming,
the creatures of winter were able to widen their lead.
When at last he arrived,
his companions told him to take aim at Fisher.

"Very well," he said, "But why kill him?"

Instead, he aimed his arrow at the Fisher's tail,
nicking the tip a bit. And that is why, even today,
every fisher's tail is shaped like a "v".

They rushed headlong after him.
But Fisher made a giant leap and vanished into the sky.
It is said that it is he who is known as the Big Dipper.
It is said, too, that if the archer refused to kill Fisher,
it was because he knew that this constellation
would one day help the future human race.
And that is why, since long ago, humans
have use the Big Dipper to find their way.

The creatures of summer resumed their chase. And soon they reached the other side of the mountain first crossed by the creatures of winter. They could hear the footsteps of the bird thieves growing fainter and fainter.

"We will never be able to catch up with them," they said. "It would be better to call out to them."

So they all began to call out:

"Winter and summer should come and go!
Winter and summer should come and go!
Each in turn should last a season!"

From far away, the voices of the others echoed in reply.
In this way, it was agreed.

At that moment the bag was opened
and the birds of summer scattered across the land.
The snow began to melt beneath the sun's warm rays.
The day had come for the world's first spring.

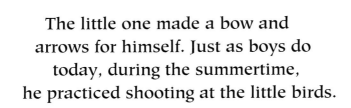

The little one made a bow and
arrows for himself. Just as boys do
today, during the summertime,
he practiced shooting at the little birds.

In the meantime, the creatures of winter
discussed how long the summertime should
last. Most of them preferred a very long
summer. Beaver wanted as many summer
moons as there were scales
on his tail. Caribou, on the other hand,
wanted as many summer moons as
there were hairs between his hooves.
But as one creature pointed out, if summer were to be
so long, winter could certainly not be any shorter!

Sapsucker listened
with an ear half-cocked,
gazing at his feet in front of him.

"*I think winter should
last six moons...*" he argued.

And well he might say so, for
Sapsucker had three toes on each foot.

This proposal met with everyone's
approval, and the creatures of winter
began their journey back.

As they were nearing home, the winter creatures were greeted
by the same two old women whom they had met at the
start of their journey. The two old women had always hoped one
day to see summer with their own eyes. Now they could no longer
contain their joy, and sang out:

"Summer is here! Summer is here!

They have brought summer to our land,

They have brought summer to our land."

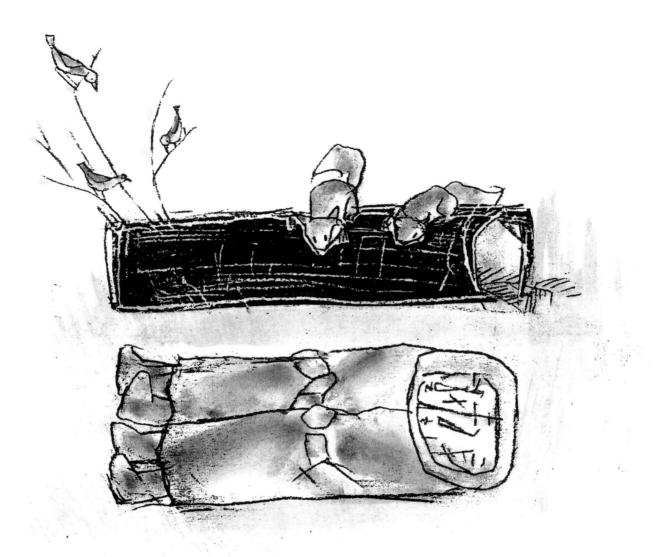

However, as soon as the two old women learned that summer would last but a season, only to be followed by winter once again, they lay down on the ground and died of old age.

They were the first two living creatures to die.

As for the little one, he continued to hunt the birds of summer
until they, worried that he would kill too many of them,
suggested that he become a bird like them. It is he,
Snow Bunting, who supposedly flies under the wing of a
Canadian goose. In this way, the little one was able to get
away and join his grandfather in eternity – now that life had begun to
move in time with the moons, the seasons and the generations.

As for the living creatures, they accepted growing old and dying, succeeded
by the younger generations.

The world, such as we know it today, had just begun.

The End.

About this story

The story that you have just read is a considerably slimmer adaptation of a longer story first reported by European travellers in the late 19th century. It was told in various forms across most of North America – among the Indians of the American West, the Canadian Northwest, the Great Lakes area, northwestern Quebec, the Ungava peninsula, and of the region extending from the mouth of the Saguenay River (Quebec) to the Atlantic coast of Labrador.[1]

In Quebec alone, in the 1960s and 1970s, Robert Lanari and Madeleine Lefebvre collected one version of this story directly from an inhabitant of Davis Inlet (Labrador).[2] Filmmaker Arthur Lamothe[3] and folklore specialist Joséphine Bacon[4] recorded further versions in Betsiamites (Quebec), as did Marie-Jeanne Basile and Gérard E. McNulty[5] in Mingan (Quebec), Sylvie Vincent[6] in Natashquan (Quebec), and Rémi Savard[7] in La Romaine and Saint-Augustin (both in Quebec). The telling of each version was the occasion of a genuine performance in the tradition that gave rise to the epic poems of Homer and Hesiod nearly 3000 years ago and that date from at least as long ago as the Bronze Age.

napeu

ishkueu

numushum

nussim

nikau

nikuss

nutau

shikuan

nipin

pupun

mush

kak

nipin
   pineshishit

atiku

utshek

nitshiku

amishku

pishimu

Mistapeo

Atshen

Innu

man

woman

my grandfather

my little one

my mother

my son

my father

sprint

summer

winter, year

moose

porcupine

small migratory
    birds

caribou

fisher

otter

beaver

month, moon, star, sun

imaginary being
    generally favourable

imaginary
    cannibal

human being

The summary version presented in this book was based on two such performances in the Innu language by François Bellefleur in La Romaine, and by Pierre Peters in Saint-Augustin. The transcriptions, which were obviously much longer, were subsequently translated by José Mailhot, Matthew Rich, Joséphine Bacon and Thérèse Roch.

As with all similar creations of the imagination, the universal concerns of man occupy centre stage – be they food, children, love, negotiations, life and death, in short, the destiny of humankind.

R. S.

1. See the research and articles published by Robert Lowie, Émile Petitot, Mentor L. William, W. Jones, W. Carson, F. G. Speck, Lucien M. Turner, Eleanor B. Leacock and Nan A. Rothschild.
2. During a legend-gathering project led by Rémi Savard in 1967 (archives of the Laboratoire d'anthropologie amérindienne no. 01-07-03-11).
3. Les Ateliers audiovisuels du Québec (A. Lamothe). Series entitled Culture amérindienne – Archives, document no. 4: "L'enfant qui avait trop de poux" undated).
4. Joséphine Bacon, archives of the Laboratoire d'anthropologie amérindienne no. 01-07-10-01.
5. Marie-Jeanne Basile and Gérard E. McNulty (collection, translation and transcription), *Atanukana. Légendes montagnaises. Montagnais Legends*, Québec City, Université Laval, Nordicana collection, Centre d'études nordiques, no. 31, 1971, pp. 27-37.
6. Sylvie Vincent, "Structures comparées du Rite et des Mythes de la Tente tremblante," *Papers of the Tenth Algonquian Conference*, Ottawa, Carleton University, 1977, pp. 90-100.
7. Rémi Savard, *Contes indiens de la basse Côte-Nord*, Ottawa, National Museums of Canada, National Museum of Man, "Mercure" collection, Canadian Ethnology Service, no. 51, 1979, pp. 38-48.